Desmond
2
Dinosaur

# Desmond Starts School

This book
belongs to

_____

*Desmond the Dinosaur Series*

Desmond is Lonely
Desmond Starts School
Desmond Goes to the Vet
Desmond and the Monsters

**HAPPY CAT BOOKS**

Published by Happy Cat Books Ltd.
Bradfield, Essex CO11 2UT, UK

This edition published 2003
1 3 5 7 9 10 8 6 4 2

A CIP catalogue record for this book is available from the British Library

ISBN 1 903285 51 8 Paperback

Printed in Poland, DRUK INTRO SA

Desmond
Dinosaur
2

# Desmond Starts School

## Althea

Illustrated by Sarah Wimperis

Happy Cat Books

Desmond woke up feeling very excited.
Today was his first day at school. He ate his
breakfast quickly and hurried off. He didn't
want to be late.

Everyone was playing in the playground.
Desmond joined in.

The school had made an extra large door, so that Desmond could get in and out. Mark had been asked to look after Desmond because he was new.

When the bell rang Mark took Desmond along to the hall.
When the children arrived, there was no room in the front row. Desmond had filled all the seats!

One of the chairs broke.
The teacher said, "Tomorrow, Desmond is going
to have to stand, or we will run out of chairs!"

Desmond enjoyed the singing a lot.

In the classroom, Mark showed Desmond his big new table, and found him a pencil.

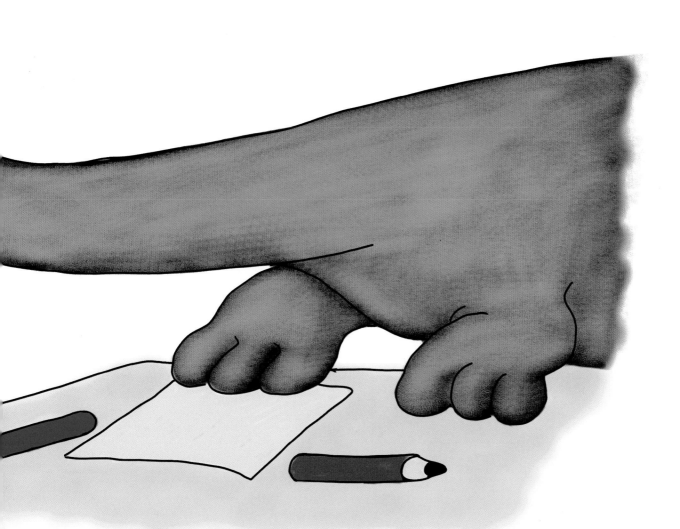

First they had a writing lesson. Desmond could write his name and quite soon he was copying lots of other words too.

It was time for P.E. Desmond liked the hoops best, but there were none left for the other children!

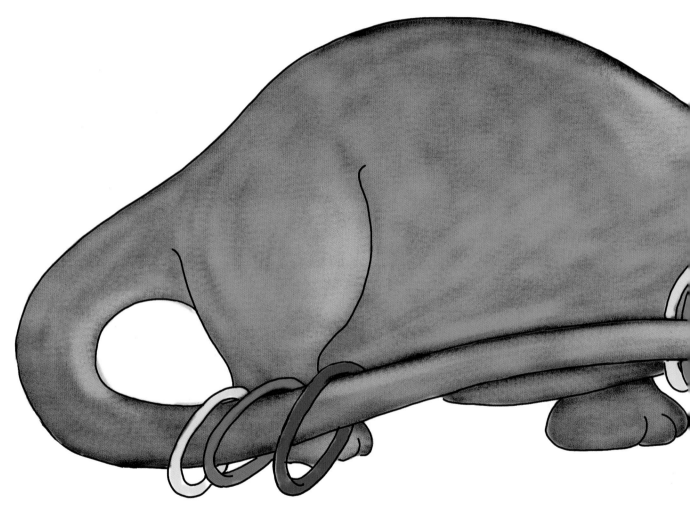

At playtime all the children wanted to play with Desmond. He thought school was great fun.

After play, Miss Baker read a story. It was all about dinosaurs, Desmond was very interested.

The bell went for dinner. Desmond ate *all* the vegetables. Some of the children were very pleased!

The teacher said, "We will have to get extra vegetables tomorrow."
"Please don't cook mine. I like them raw," said Desmond.

After dinner, everyone went on the bus to the swimming pool. Desmond rode on top.

SWIMMING POOL

Desmond was kind at the pool.
Everyone took it in turns to
have a ride on his back.

Then Desmond dived into the pool. He made the water splash everywhere.
Miss Baker thought it would take a bit of time to get used to having a dinosaur in her school.

Back at school again, the last lesson was reading. Desmond could only manage the easy words.

Soon it was time to go home.
Desmond felt a bit sad. Everyone
said, "Please come back tomorrow."

"I will go to school again and again, until I can read properly," Desmond said to himself, as he walked home.

With many thanks to Mark Cooper, who, when aged 7, inspired this story.